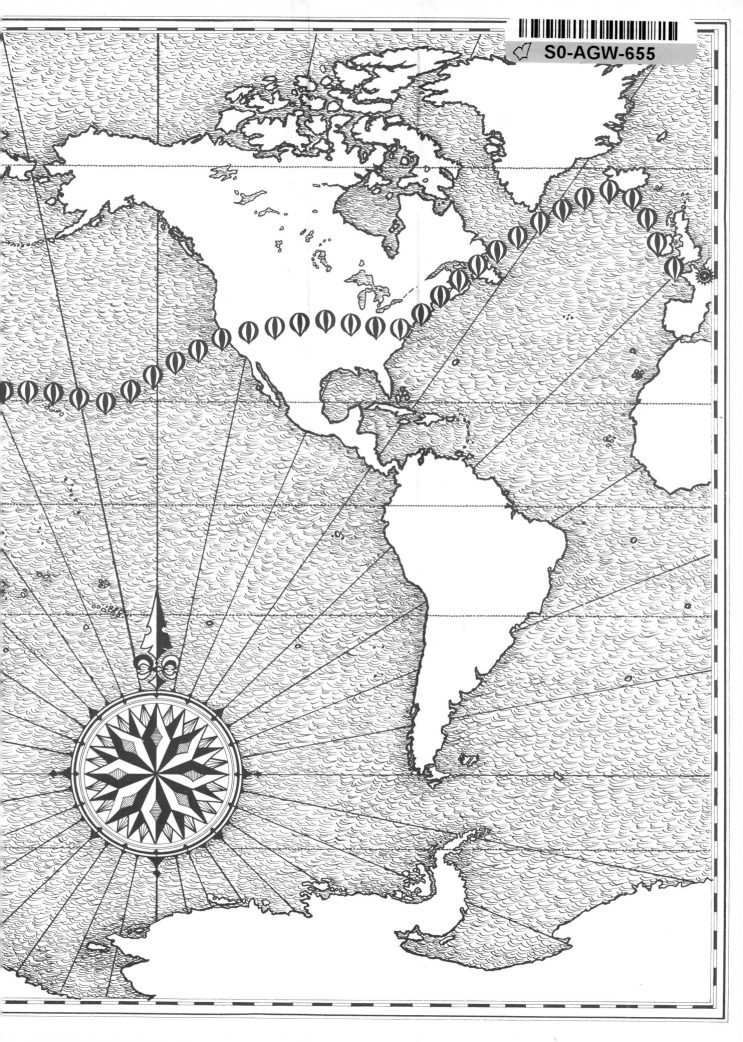

THE GREAT ROUND-THE-WORLD BALLOON RACE

SUE SCULLARD

DUTTON CHILDREN'S BOOKS

NEW YORK

Library of Congress Cataloging-in-Publication Data
Scullard, Sue.
  The great round-the-world balloon race /
Sue Scullard.—1st American ed.
    p. cm.
  "Originally published in Great Britain 1990
by Macmillan Children's Books"—T.p. verso.
  Summary: The adventures of Harriet Shaw and her
niece and nephew, Rebecca and William, as they
set out on a round-the-world balloon race.
  ISBN 0-525-44692-3
  [1. Balloon ascensions—Fiction.
2. Voyages and travels—Fiction.] I. Title.
PZ7.S43744Gr 1991
[E]—dc20   90-40590 CIP AC

First published in the United States 1991 by
Dutton Children's Books,
a division of Penguin Books USA Inc.

Originally published in Great Britain 1990 by
Macmillan Children's Books, London.

First American Edition   Printed in Italy
10 9 8 7 6 5 4 3 2 1

Harriet Shaw, the famous balloonist, put down her sewing and looked at Rebecca and William.

"I can't wait to finish this," she sighed. "I'm dying for another adventure. But what will it be?"

Her niece and nephew thought for a while. "I know," Rebecca said suddenly. "How about a balloon race?"

"You could go all the way around the world," suggested William.

"A round-the-world race!" exclaimed Aunt Harriet. "What a wonderful idea! I know lots of balloonists who will jump at the chance. Isabelle and Mohammed and Angus and..."

"Can't we please come with you?" asked William.

"It *was* our idea," said Rebecca.

"Well, I don't know...." said their aunt. "Ballooning can be dangerous, and it's very hard work. You'd have to help write up the log, read the maps, keep lookout...."

"Yes, yes!" yelled the children. "We will!"

And that was how it all began.

A CHALLENGE
TO ALL BALLOONISTS

You Are Invited To Enter

THE FIRST

ROUND-THE-WORLD
BALLOON
RACE

STARTING IN PARIS ON 21st NOVEMBER

The Anniversary of the First Manned Flight in 1783

The route covers the following points: the Black Forest of Germany, the Swiss Alps, the Mediterranean Sea, the Nile Valley, the Arabian Desert, the Makran coast, the Indian Desert, the Himalaya Mountains, the jungle of the Irrawaddy, the rain forests of Borneo, the Pacific Islands, the Hawaiian Islands, the Colorado plateaus, New York City, the northern Atlantic Ocean, the southern coast of England, and Paris.   TOTAL DISTANCE: 23,000 miles.

RULES

1. Competitors must follow the route described above.
2. Only gas and hot-air balloons are permitted.
3. Any contact with the ground will disqualify competitors.
4. Competitors enter at their own risk. They should be prepared for extremely high altitudes, very hot and very cold weather, and the possibility of balloon failure.

THE COMPETITORS

FIREBREATHER

William, Aunt Harriet, and Rebecca

U.S.A.

SNOWS OF FUJI

Hiroki

Japan

LOCH LOMOND

Angus

Scotland

TRIOMPHE

Isabelle

France

KIWI

Aroha

New Zealand

VILLAGER

Hans

Denmark

NORTHERN STAR

Naomi

Canada

CRESCENT MOON

Mohammed

Egypt

DAYBREAK

Maximilian

Germany

KALEIDOSCOPE

Rick and Jimmy

Great Britain

FOLLOW THEIR PROGRESS IN THE RACE.

At last the big day arrived. As the band played and the crowd cheered, dozens of balloons rose into the sky above Paris. The race had begun!

"There are so many balloons that I can't even count them," said Rebecca. "Do you think *Firebreather* can beat them all?"

"Someone has to win," said Aunt Harriet. "It might as well be us. We're off!"

The contestants stayed close together for the first three hundred miles. But as they passed over the Black Forest, it began to hail. "Look," said William as he watched some balloons descend. "A few people are already in trouble."

The balloons flew over Italy and across the Mediterranean to the Sahara Desert, where clouds of dust whirled through the air. "I can only see Naomi, Isabelle, and Hiroki," said Rebecca. "Have the others dropped out already?"

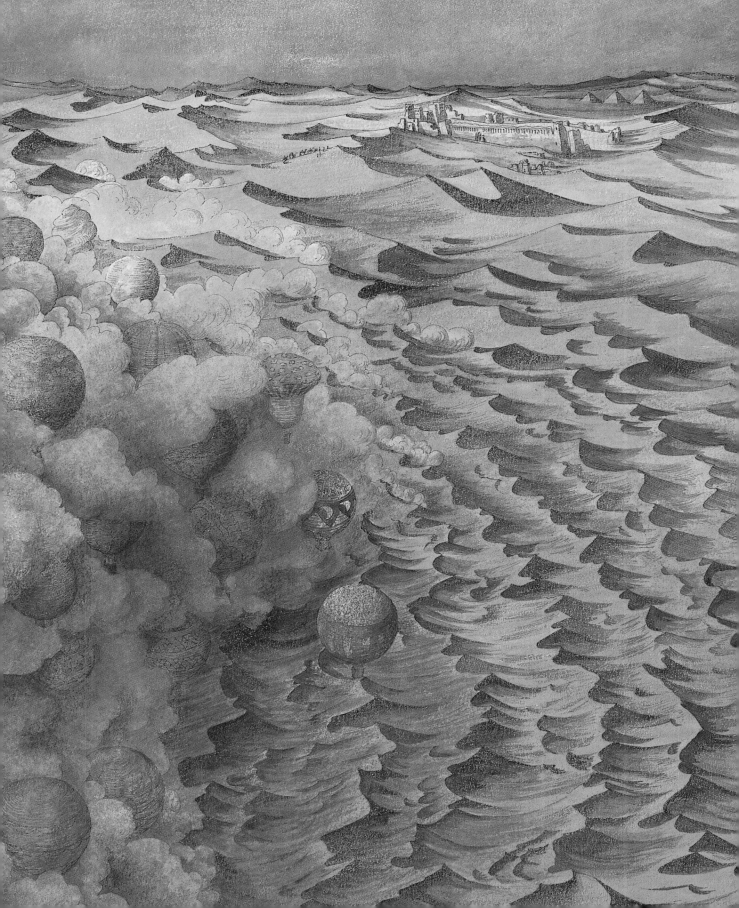

They hadn't. With the dusty desert air behind them, many
balloons were visible again. "We'll need more altitude if we're
going to clear those mountains," said Aunt Harriet. "Can you
please stop waving at Maximilian for a minute and find our
oxygen masks?"

Rebecca and William did, and *Firebreather* began to rise.
"Some of the balloonists are going down, not up," said William.

"Their oxygen masks may be clogged with dust from the storm,"
said Aunt Harriet. "I'm glad we kept ours in the trunk. Good
thinking, you two."

Rebecca and William gasped at the view as the balloon rose higher. "Those are the Himalayas—'the roof of the world,'" said Aunt Harriet, her voice muffled by the oxygen mask.

"Will we make it over the top?" asked William.

"Sure we will!" said Rebecca.

But not all the contestants did. Rick and Jimmy began to descend—it looked as if the stitching on *Kaleidoscope* wouldn't hold. "Isabelle's not going to make it either," said William.

"What a shame," said Aunt Harriet. "There's so much more scenery and excitement to come."

The crew of *Firebreather* got more excitement than they bargained for in the steamy Burmese jungle. Aunt Harriet took the balloon down low so the children could get a closer look at the wild animals. Rebecca leaned out to take a picture...and almost became a crocodile's lunch!

They were crossing the lush forests of Borneo when William said, "I can still see *Crescent Moon* and *Villager*—and I think that's *Loch Lomond* behind us."

"All I see in front of us is a lot of smoke," said Rebecca.

"Smoke?" exclaimed Aunt Harriet. "My goodness, it's coming from that mountain! We have to warn the others."

"Look out!" they shouted as loud as they could. "Volcano ahead!"

Suddenly, flames shot from the mouth of the smoking volcano. The balloonists who were nearest to the volcano had no choice but to abandon the race. Rebecca and William spotted Angus and Naomi parachuting to the ground. "If it weren't for you, Rebecca, we'd be out of the race too," said Aunt Harriet.

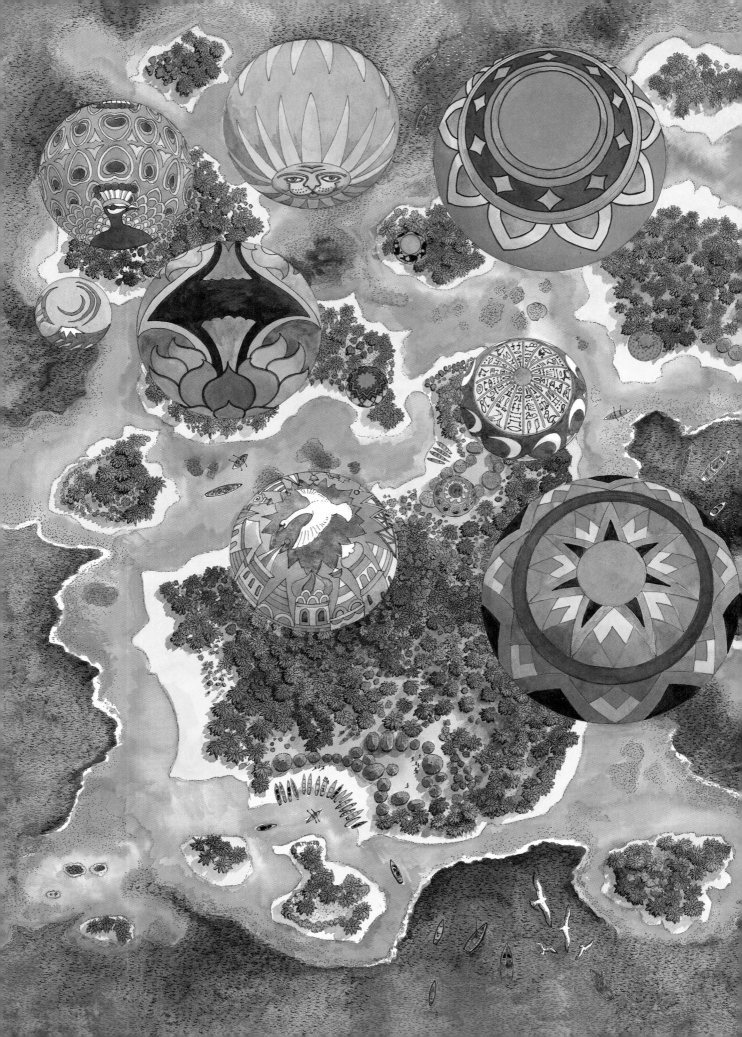

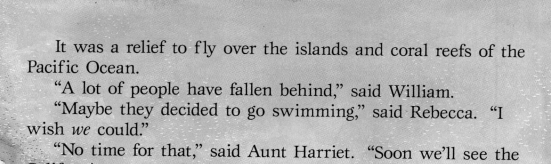

It was a relief to fly over the islands and coral reefs of the Pacific Ocean.

"A lot of people have fallen behind," said William.

"Maybe they decided to go swimming," said Rebecca. "I wish *we* could."

"No time for that," said Aunt Harriet. "Soon we'll see the California coast and begin to cross America."

As *Firebreather* flew east, both William and Rebecca were thrilled by their first glimpse of the Grand Canyon. "Fantastic!" said Rebecca.

"Watch out for tricky air currents," said Aunt Harriet.

"And for airplanes," added William. "Look!"

Vintage airplanes were flying through the canyon, diving, climbing, and doing stunts. Some of the other balloonists were so busy watching the planes that they forgot to watch where they were going.

Rain was pouring down when the balloons reached New York City, and more competitors dropped out of the race. "Everyone's getting tired," said Aunt Harriet. "We've flown about twenty thousand miles."

"We can't quit now," said William. "We're going to win. Right, Rebecca?"

Rebecca didn't answer. She was fast asleep.

Huge icicles formed on the balloons as they flew through the arctic cold over the northern Atlantic Ocean.

"The weight of the icicles is pulling some people down," said William. "*Villager*'s almost grounded on that gigantic iceberg."

"*Kiwi*'s gone down, too," said Rebecca. "That leaves just Maximilian and us. We've *got* to beat him to Paris."

But *Daybreak* was in the lead as they flew over England.

"There's only one way to catch up, and that's to lighten the load," said Aunt Harriet. "I know you can manage on your own."

And before they could answer, she climbed over the side of the basket.

"Good luck!" she called as she parachuted to earth. "You can do it!"

With William and Rebecca at the helm, *Firebreather* slowly but steadily cut *Daybreak*'s lead. "We're gaining on him," said William. "Look! I think his balloon is leaking."

Sure enough, *Daybreak* began to lose altitude. The children watched as Maximilian finally landed his balloon in a field—just outside Paris.

"There's the Eiffel Tower!" cried Rebecca.

"Yippee!" yelled William. "Three cheers for *Firebreather,* the best balloon in the race—and the world!"

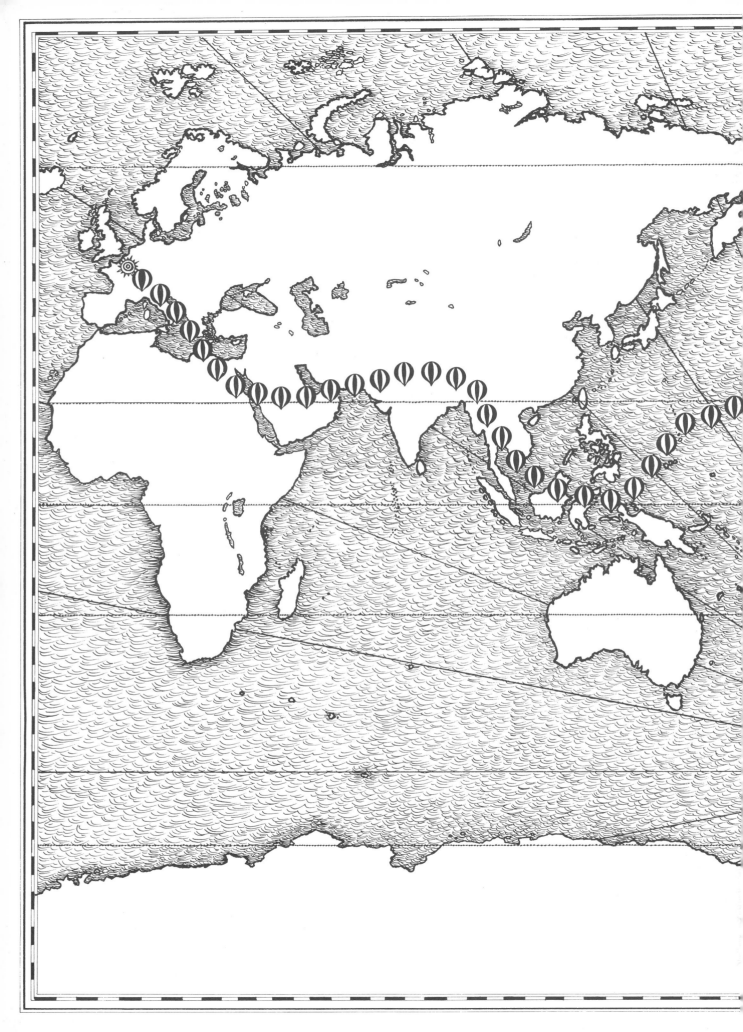